For Louisa Wright Krauss,
otherwise known as Lulu
—T.K.

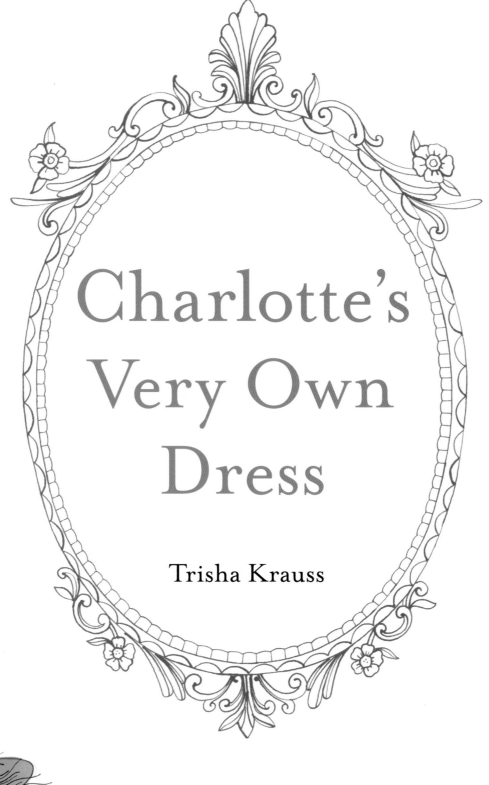

Charlotte's Very Own Dress

Trisha Krauss

Random House 🏠 New York

Mr. and Mrs. Bartlett-Kruger had six little girls.

Gwendolyn was the oldest. Next came Winifred, followed closely by Ruth, and then the twins, Amelia and Cordelia.

Last of all was Charlotte.

Having five older sisters was usually a good thing, decided Charlotte. It was particularly useful for playing musical chairs, and there was always one sister or another to amuse her.

Best of all, Charlotte got to keep all of her sisters' outgrown toys.

Charlotte rescued these toys and tended them with care.
Adding a stitch here, a bit of cotton there, and perhaps a dab
of paste, she made these abandoned toys much better than new.

Although Charlotte loved her big sisters very much, the one bad thing about being the youngest was . . .

Charlotte got stuck with her sisters'
hand-me-down clothes.

One day Mr. and Mrs. Bartlett-Kruger announced that they were going to throw a fancy dress-up party.

The sisters shouted with glee and jumped in the air as they sang, "We will wear pretty dresses, dance the fandango, the cha-cha, the Charleston, and the tango!"

Dresses are never pretty by the time they are passed down to me, thought Charlotte sadly.

On the day of the party, the house was abuzz.
Lanterns were hung, flowers were arranged,
and canapés, cakes, and custards were prepared.

The Bartlett crystal was shined and the Kruger silver polished while the girls prepared their party dresses.

Gwendolyn gushed over her
new pink gown adorned with
grosgrain ribbons.

Winifred wondered if Gwendolyn's old woolen wrap
would look better on herself than it had on her big sister.

Ruth was ravishing in last year's raspberry silk.

The twins chittered and chattered as they dressed in Winifred
and Ruth's old taffeta tunics and patent-leather shoes.

Amid the flurry of party preparation, Charlotte woefully
awaited the procession of five well-intentioned sisters
offering five worn-out dresses.

First came Gwendolyn with an ancient frock in hand.

"Look," she cooed, "this dress suits you to a tee."

Then came Winifred and Ruth
with last year's party dresses.

"If I could cut your hair *ever
so slightly,* you would look like a
film star in this polka-dot silk,"
said Winifred, scissors ready.

"Oh, how I hate to part with this
dress, but it would look *far* nicer
on you than it did on any of us,"
said Ruth, rather too enthusiastically.

And when the twins turned up
with two tattered old numbers . . .

Charlotte collapsed in a heap and
started to sob. Then she drifted into
fretful slumber. . . .

Gwendolyn gathered the girls and declared, "None of these dresses will do!
Charlotte always fixes up our old toys and makes them better than new.
With a stitch here, a bit of ribbon there, and perhaps a feather or two,
we can make Charlotte her very own dress."

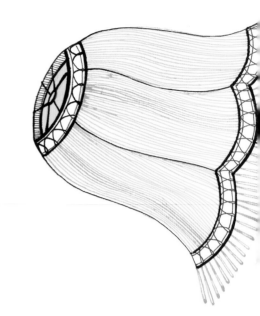

They collected all of their old dresses and picked up items from around the house.

While the clock was ticking and Charlotte was sleeping,
five kindhearted sisters worked without rest.

Charlotte woke
with a start as a cello
struck a chord.

To her amazement, hanging in her
wardrobe was the most extraordinary dress.

She dressed in a hurry; there was no time to waste.

Charlotte's heart skipped a beat as she
made her grand entrance.

For her dress was made not
only of hand-me-down garments,
but with sisterly love.